Say What, Little Duck?

Say What, Little Duck?

Written by: Jennifer Teschendorf

Illustrated by: Sarah Cazee-Widhalm

Mill City Press, Inc.
2301 Lucien Way #415
Maitland, FL 32751
407.339.4217
www.millcitypress.net

© 2021 by Jen Teschendorf

Illustrated by: Sarah Cazee-Widhalm

Paperback ISBN-13: 978-1-66281-287-3
Hardcover ISBN-13: 978-1-66281-288-0
Ebook ISBN-13: 978-1-66281-289-7

For my little duck, Harper Colleen.

Once there was a little duck, who only liked to "QUACK!"

His momma would try to talk to him, but he never could talk back.

She would
ask if he
was hungry,
or if he
wanted to
play outside.

She would
ask if he
was sleepy,
or if he
wanted to go
for a ride.

Little Duck had lots to say,
but the words wouldn't come out right!

So all he said was, "QUACK QUACK QUACK"
all morning, noon, and night.

One day his momma had a thought, to help her baby boy;
she picked out all his favorite things that brought him lots of joy.

She started in the kitchen when it was time for him to eat,
and offered him some "QUACKERS" as a tasty little treat.

Little Duck thought that was silly!
QUACKERS wasn't right!

He thought about it carefully and said,
"CRRRACKERS" with all his might!

Momma Duck was thrilled and she wanted to have more fun.

She brought Little Duck his favorite book
about farm animals in the sun.

When they reached the rooster page Momma cried,
"QUACK-A-DOODLE-DOO!"

Little Duck giggled and said, "NOOO!!"
which made Momma happy too.

Once she got him started, Little Duck just wouldn't stop!

He talked and talked and talked and talked until he finally dropped.

Momma tucked her baby in and whispered really low,

"You're my favorite little duck
and I will always love you so."

We would like to give a special thanks to our amazing friends and family who have encouraged us to chase our dreams.

To Tom, Colleen, Morgan, and Jeff; this book would not be possible without you.

Thank you for lending an ear, hand, and shoulder during this entire process.

About the Author

Jen Teschendorf lives in the Twin Cities with her husband, daughter, and their beloved dog, Rudy. She attended the University of Montana with the aspirations of learning how to make movies, but left with the artistry of telling a great story.

Jen typically can be found writing children's books, editing photos, or making short movies - but only after her little duck goes to sleep!

About the Illustrator

Sarah Cazee-Widhalm is a Montana born and raised artist currently residing in the beautiful Pacific Northwest. She attended the University of Montana in Missoula where she became lifelong friends with the author of this book, and earned a Bachelor of Fine Arts in Painting.

In addition to making art, she enjoys woodworking and blacksmithing at her rural homestead where she lives with her wife, two dogs, two cats, and a multitude of wild animals.

CPSIA information can be obtained
at www.ICGtesting.com
Printed in the USA
BVHW061037290421
606136BV00006B/634

9 781662 812873